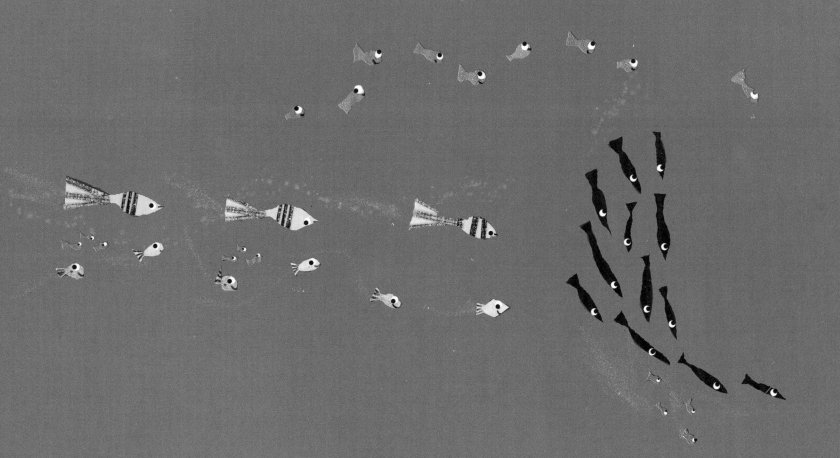

For Mam and Dad.

Starfish Bay® Children's Books
An imprint of Starfish Bay Publishing
www.starfishbaypublishing.com

THE SALMON OF KNOWLEDGE

© Celina Buckley, 2019
ISBN 978-1-76036-070-2
First Published 2019
Printed in China by Beijing Shangtang Print & Packaging Co., Ltd.
11 Tengren Road, Niulanshan Town, Shunyi District, Beijing, China

Celina Buckley grew up on a farm in the middle of the countryside in County Cork, Ireland. She earned her Bachelor of Education (Hons) from Mary Immaculate College, Limerick, in 2011. For the following four years, she enjoyed working as a primary school teacher and reading many children's books with the children of St. Joseph's Primary School, Macroom, County Cork. She then decided to take a break from primary school teaching to pursue her life-long passion for drawing and children's literature and embarked upon the Masters in Children's Books Illustration at the Cambridge School of Art.

The Salmon of Knowledge

Retold and Illustrated by

Celina Buckley

The Salmon of Knowledge is a traditional Irish Legend,
which has been passed down from generation to generation.

Long ago in a deep, dark forest,
nine hazel trees grew over an
ancient well of wisdom.

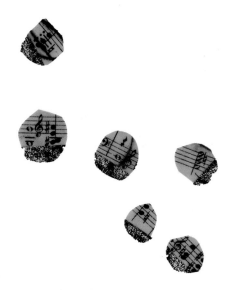

One day, the wind blew nine hazelnuts into the well,
and an ordinary salmon
swallowed them all up.

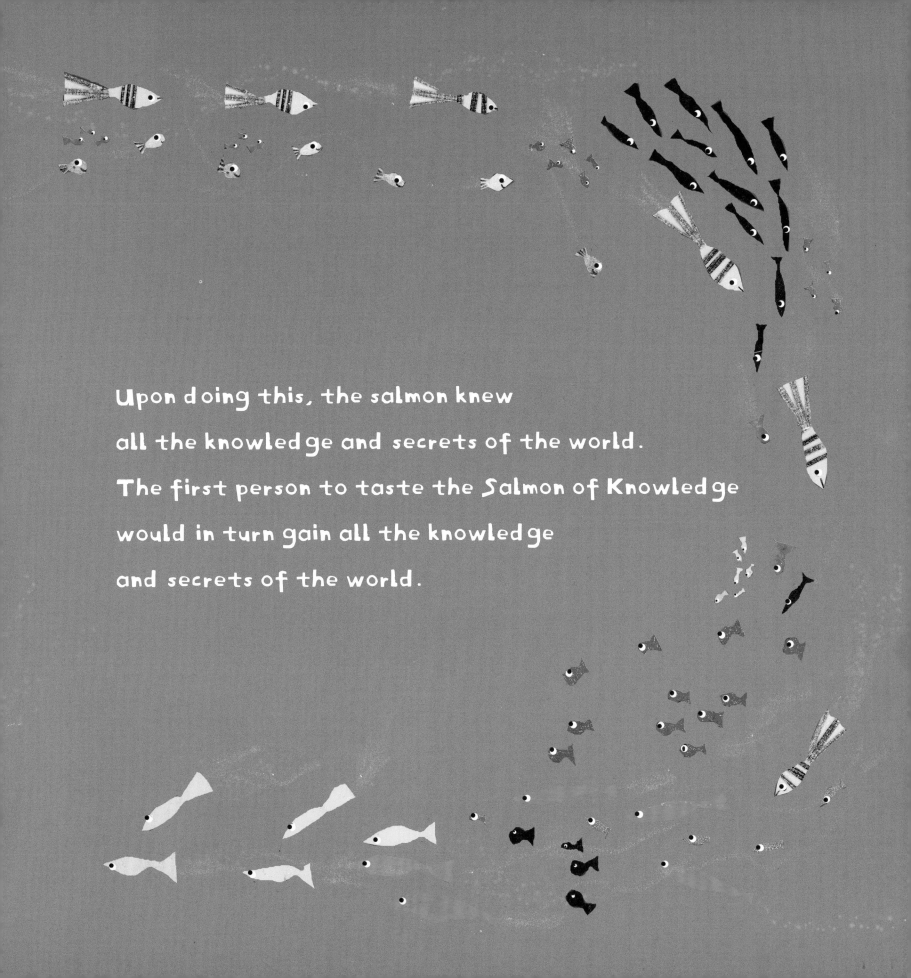

Upon doing this, the salmon knew
all the knowledge and secrets of the world.
The first person to taste the Salmon of Knowledge
would in turn gain all the knowledge
and secrets of the world.

Over the years,
many people heard
about the **Salmon of Knowledge**.

But nobody could ever find it.

A wise poet named Finnegas

wanted to catch the Salmon of Knowledge, too.

He was considered to be one of the wisest men in the land.
Despite this, he was still determined to know all
the knowledge and secrets of the world.

He made his home beside the river and spent most of his days trying to catch the Salmon of Knowledge.

One day, as Finnegas was fishing, he noticed a young boy walking by the edge of the forest.

His name was Fionn.

He wanted to become a great warrior.

If a boy had not been taught by an elderly poet,
he was not considered a warrior.

Finnegas agreed to teach Fionn, but
he never told him about the
Salmon of Knowledge.

Over the years, Finnegas showed Fionn
HOW TO BECOME A WARRIOR.

While Fionn learned these skills,
Finnegas never stopped searching for
the Salmon of Knowledge.

HOW TO BECOME A WARRIOR

Jump over a branch as tall as yourself.

Race through the forest without breaking a twig.

Pull a thorn out of your foot while running.

Learn twelve books of poetry off by heart.

Defend yourself against nine warriors while buried waist high, with just a shield and a hazelstick.

Run under a branch as high as your knees.

Take no dowry with a wife.

One morning, a flicker of orange
rippled across the smooth waters of the river.

Finnegas jumped to his feet. The wait was over. The salmon had come.

He crawled to the water's edge.

Holding his breath, he dipped his fishing rod deeper
into the riverbed. With a sharp crack,
his fishing rod bent, and
the salmon was his.

Finnegas was exhausted after catching the salmon.
He asked Fionn to clean and cook the salmon and to wake him up
when it was ready.

He warned Fionn not to taste the salmon until after
he'd had the first bite.
Then he promised they would share a fine meal together.

This seemed fair to Fionn, and
he began preparing the meal
straightaway.

Not long after Fionn begun cooking the fish, he noticed a blister bubbling through the scales.

Without thinking, he pressed his thumb hard on it and burst it.

With a sharp cry of pain, he sucked on his thumb to soothe the burn.

Fionn continued to cook. When the salmon was ready, he woke Finnegas.

Finnegas had waited a long time for this moment
and quickly ate a piece of salmon.

To his surprise he didn't feel any different or wiser.

Finnegas looked at Fionn and noticed something strange about him.

He asked him if he had eaten any of the salmon and
Fionn said he hadn't, just as he had asked.

When Finnegas asked if he had tasted even a tiny bit
of the salmon, Fionn suddenly remembered the blister.

Finnegas's heart sank with disappointed as he heard Fionn's words.

Finnegas could not teach
Fionn anything more than he
already knew. So, Fionn packed up his things
and thanked Finnegas for all his help. Fionn became
the greatest and most knowledgeable warrior
in all the land.

From that day on, the story of
Fionn and the Salmon of Knowledge
spread across the roaming hills
and deep glens, where it is said
the nine trees grow above the
well to this very day.